CW00516442

CHRISTMAS HITS
Playalong *for* Flute

WISE PUBLICATIONS
London/New York/Paris/Sydney/Copenhagen/Madrid/Tokyo

Exclusive Distributors:
Music Sales Limited
8/9 Frith Street, London W1V 5TZ, England.
Music Sales Pty Limited
120 Rothschild Avenue, Rosebery, NSW 2018, Australia.

Order No. AM966944
ISBN 0-7119-8436-0
This book © Copyright 2000 by Wise Publications.

Book design by Michael Bell Design.
Music arranged by Paul Honey.
Music processed by Enigma Music Production Services.
Cover photography by George Taylor.
Printed in the United Kingdom by Page Bros., Norwich, Norfolk.

CD produced by Paul Honey.
Instrumental solos by John Whelan.
Engineered by Kester Sims.

Your Guarantee of Quality:
As publishers, we strive to produce every book to
the highest commercial standards.
The music has been freshly engraved and the book has been
carefully designed to minimise awkward page turns and
to make playing from it a real pleasure.
Particular care has been given to specifying acid-free, neutral-sized
paper made from pulps which have not been elemental chlorine bleached.
This pulp is from farmed sustainable forests and was
produced with special regard for the environment.
Throughout, the printing and binding have been planned to
ensure a sturdy, attractive publication which should give years of enjoyment.
If your copy fails to meet our high standards,
please inform us and we will gladly replace it.

Music Sales' complete catalogue describes thousands of
titles and is available in full colour sections by subject,
direct from Music Sales Limited.
Please state your areas of interest and send a
cheque/postal order for £1.50 for postage to:
Music Sales Limited, Newmarket Road, Bury St. Edmunds, Suffolk IP33 3YB.

www.musicsales.com

GuestSpot

Fingering Guide

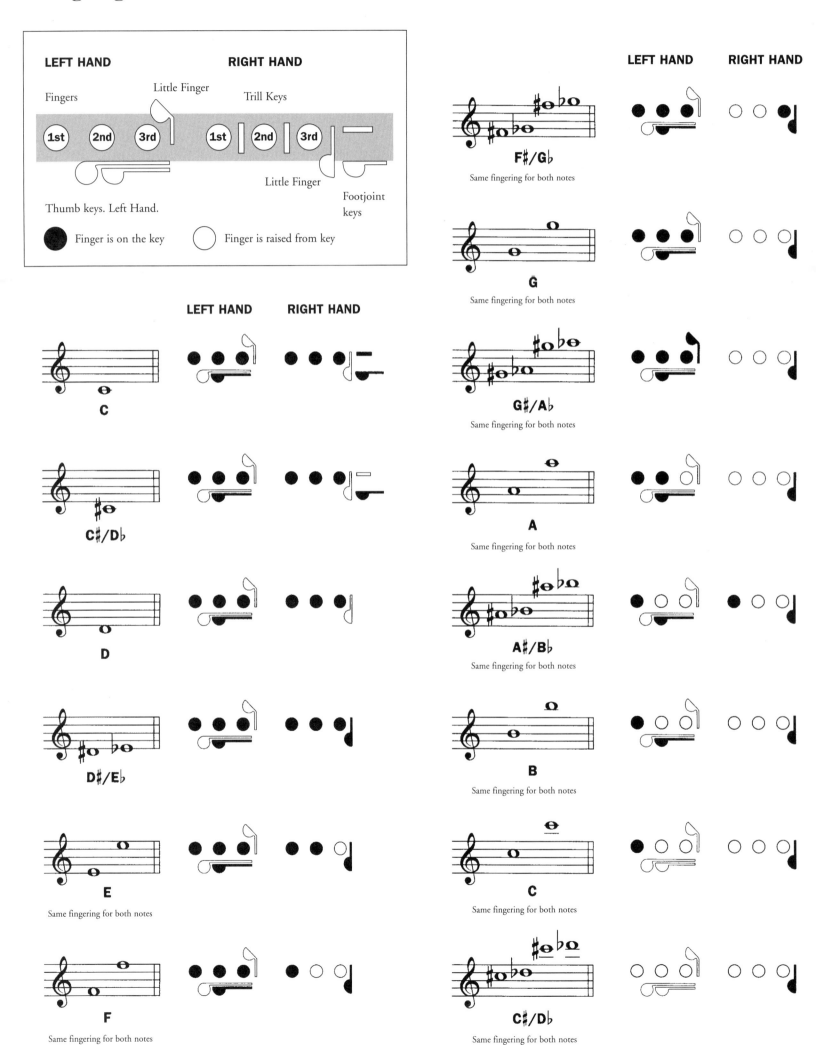

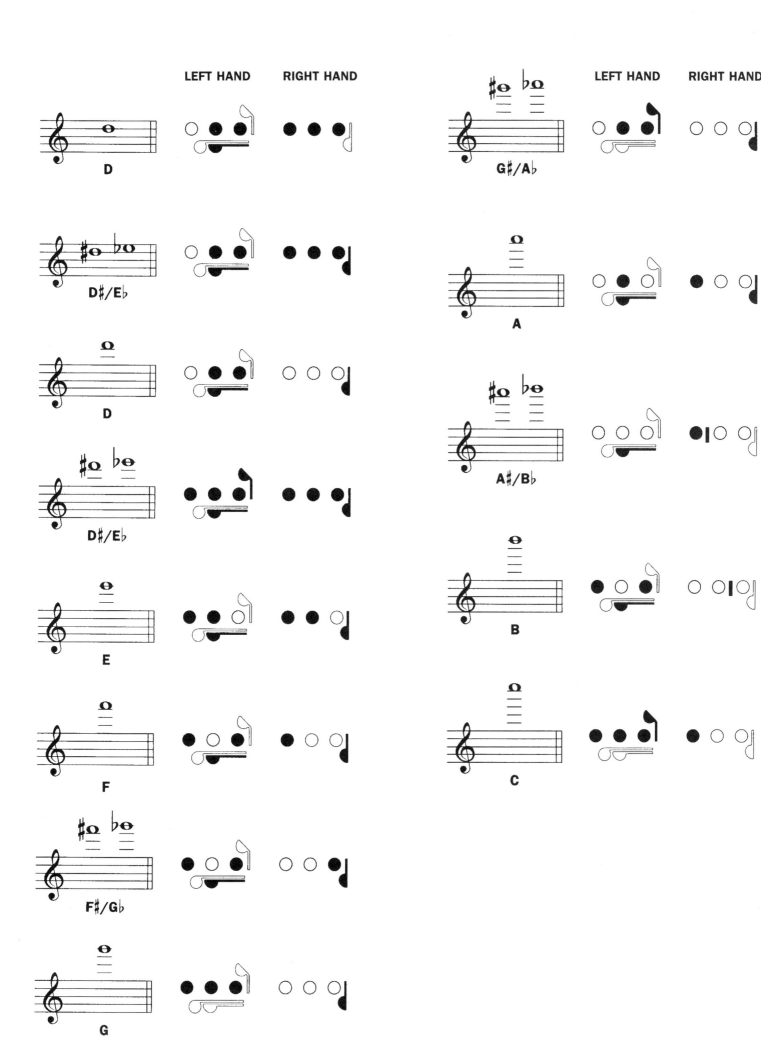

Fairytale Of New York

Words & Music by Shane MacGowan & Jem Finer

Happy Xmas (War Is Over)

Words & Music by John Lennon & Yoko Ono

I Believe In Father Christmas

Words & Music by Peter Sinfield & Greg Lake

Moderately

I Wish It Could Be Christmas Every Day

Words & Music by Roy Wood

molto rall.

Lonely This Christmas

Words & Music by Mike Chapman & Nicky Chinn

Mistletoe And Wine

Words by Leslie Stewart & Jeremy Paul
Music by Keith Strachan

Merry Xmas Everybody

Words & Music by Neville Holder & James Lea

poco rall.

Stop The Cavalry

Words & Music by Jona Lewie

Wonderful Christmastime

Words & Music by Paul McCartney

Brightly

A Spaceman Came Travelling

Words & Music by Chris De Burgh

Moderately

9/07 (63363)